Be Home in Time for Supper

Nicholas Bozza

Fulton Books, Inc.
Meadville, PA

Published by Fulton Books 2020

ISBN 978-1-64952-342-6 (paperback)
ISBN 978-1-64952-343-3 (digital)

Printed in the United States of America

n memory of my amazing parents, Carmen and Mary Jean, who showed me what family was all about.

When I was a little boy, I lived in a little house in a little town and went to a little school.

Every morning, Mama would wake me up and say, "Come on, angel. It's time for school."

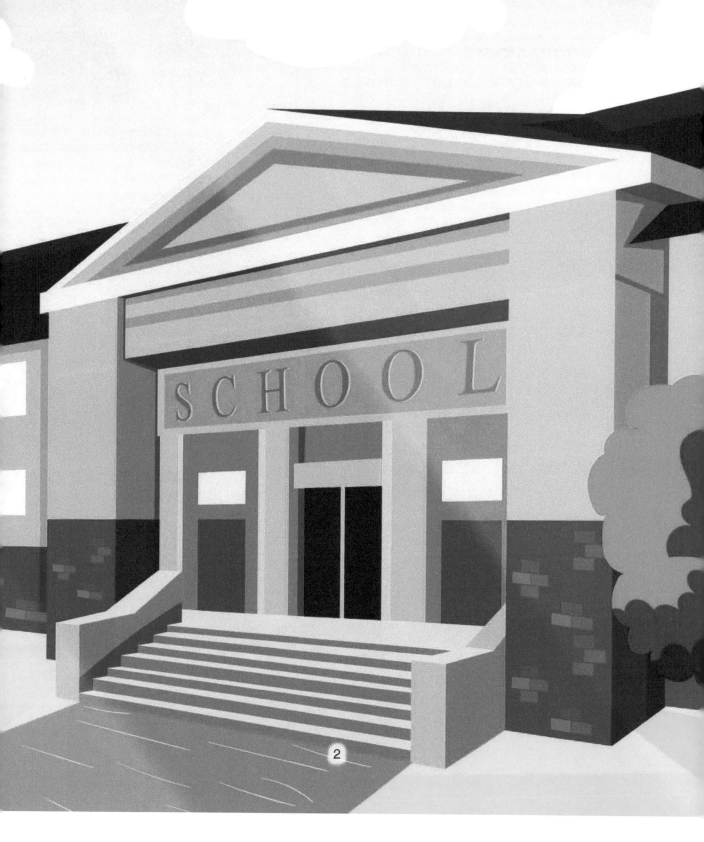

My two big brothers would always complain about having to get up, and my little baby brother didn't have to go to school yet, so he stayed in bed. But I loved going to school, so I always got dressed and ate breakfast.

When I was finished eating, I would brush my teeth and put my coat on so that I could walk to school. Mama and I said our prayers, and she would always kiss me on the forehead. "Have a good day," she would say.

When I left for school, Mama would stand on the porch and wave goodbye, and sometimes she would blow kisses to me.

After school, I walked home with my friends. As I went into the house, I could smell my dinner cooking. Oh, how hungry it always made me! Mama loved to cook, and she always made yummy things to eat.

"Just a little longer before we eat," Mama would say. "Daddy will be home in time for supper."

My daddy worked in a factory, and when he came home, he was always really tired. But even though he was tired, he always made a fuss about us. I loved it when he came home.

Every day, when I came home from school, I had to do my homework first. I didn't like math, but Mama would sit with me and try to help me understand it. When my homework was done, I would ask if I could go outside to play with my friends Bobby, Skippy, and Craig.

Mama would say, "You can go, angel, but be home in time for supper."

I loved it when she called me angel.

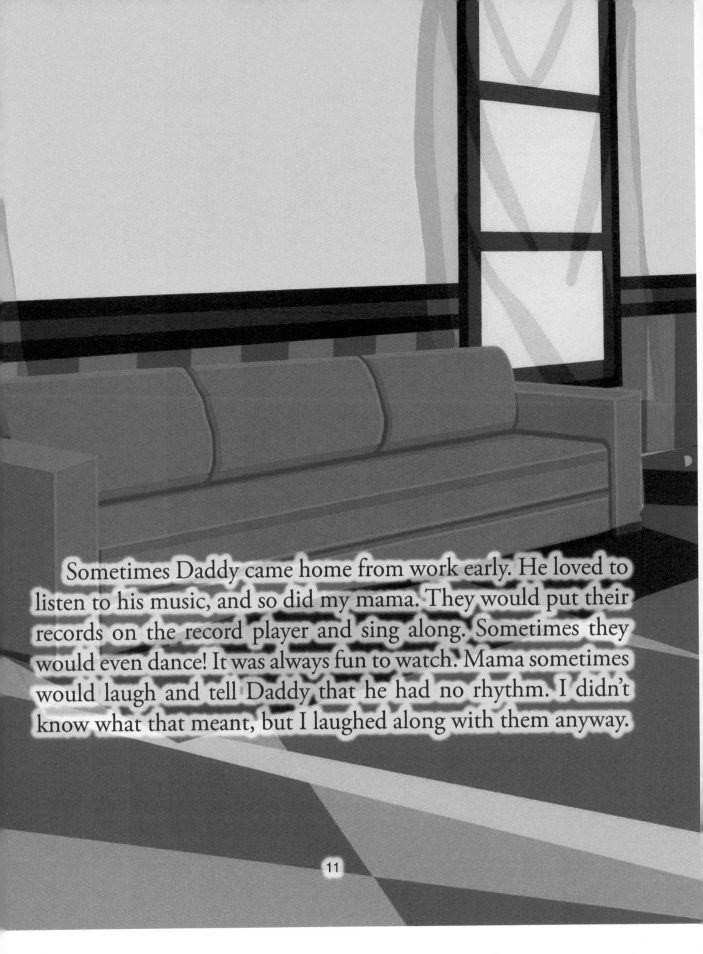

Sometimes Daddy came home from work early. He loved to listen to his music, and so did my mama. They would put their records on the record player and sing along. Sometimes they would even dance! It was always fun to watch. Mama sometimes would laugh and tell Daddy that he had no rhythm. I didn't know what that meant, but I laughed along with them anyway.

Once a week, the cargo trains would pass through my town and follow the track on Atlantic Avenue. Daddy would take me to watch the train go by, and I loved it.

Before we went, Mama would wipe her hands on her apron and said, "Okay, you two, just be home in time for supper."

Daddy used to hold my hand and tell me that when I become a big boy, I could ride the trains. I only want to ride the trains if I could ride with my daddy. We'll have fun—yes, we will!

Mama and Daddy went to the grocery store every Friday night. Sometimes I would go with them. While Mama went to shop, Daddy and I walked around the store. Daddy sometimes bought me a toy, and once in a while, he let me pick out my favorite ice cream. Mama said that we could eat the ice cream when we got home. I loved going to the store with Mama and Daddy.

On Sundays, we always had a big family dinner, and my aunts and uncles and cousins would come over. Sometimes before dinner, I would ride my bike around the neighborhood with my cousins Anthony, Joey, and Ralphie. Then we would stop at our corner store and buy penny candy. I liked the red gummy fish the best!

"Have fun and don't eat too many sweets," Mama would say.
"And you boys make sure to be home in time for supper."
"We sure will, Mama!"

At bedtime, Mama would tuck me in and say prayers with me. She would kiss me good night and then turn on my night-light before she left the room. Then Daddy would come in and kiss me good night. Daddy had all kinds of stubble on his face and would rub it on my cheek. It hurt a little, but we would laugh and laugh. I loved it when he did that.

My mama and daddy loved me. Daddy always said, "Someday, son, you're going to be president of the United States."

I didn't want to be the president because I wanted to be just like my mama and daddy. They were superheroes to me, and I want to be one too. Besides, I think that being a superhero would be more fun than being the president. A superhero is strong and smart, and they don't have to go to bed early at night. If I was a superhero, I would help people but would always remember to be home in time for supper.

I told Mama and Daddy that when I am a big boy, I want to take care of them when they are old. I want them to know that they could count on me too. I mean, even though I will be a big boy, I will still be their little boy. And if they want to go outside, I'll make sure to tell them to be home in time for supper.

CPSIA information can be obtained
at www.ICGtesting.com
Printed in the USA
LVHW072004280521
688829LV00001B/12